About the Author

I am a wife, mother of two sons, a grandmother to three beautiful grandchildren and have two golden doodle dogs. I spent my working life as a secretary and in my spare time enjoyed amateur dramatics and singing. Now, in my retirement, I am lucky to live part of my life on the west of the Isle of Wight and the rest at my home in Swadlincote, South Derbyshire. For a few years I have enjoyed writing rhymes, usually very short, silly ones and that's how Philomena came to be.

Philomena the Fairy

A CIP catalogue record for this title is
available from the British Library.
ISBN 978-1-83875-257-6

*Nightingale Books is an imprint of
Pegasus Elliot MacKenzie Publishers Ltd.*
www.pegasuspublishers.com

First Published in 2021

Nightingale Books
Sheraton House Castle Park
Cambridge England

Printed & Bound in Great Britain

Cherril Prentice

Philomena the Fairy

Nightingale Books

Philomena the fairy was exceedingly pretty,
She was kind, she was sweet, she was clever and witty.

Her clothes were all pink and frilly and shiny
And she lived in a house that was spotless, but tiny.

She longed for a house that was covered in flowers,
Three storeys high with turrets and towers.

She'd never afford one so she'd tried to use magic,
But unfortunately this turned out to be tragic.

Her problem, you see, was her wand was no good,
It simply was crooked with a knot in the wood.

The star at the top was a little bit droopy
And it made Philomena look decidedly loopy.

However she tried, it always backfired
And poor Philomena got terribly tired.

She pointed her wand and said a 'house spell'
But, oh deary me, she didn't do well.

She pointed her wand and said, "This cannot fail."
But horror of horrors, she aimed at a snail.

Imagine its shock when it grew a big shell
With turrets and towers and flowers as well.

It gave her a look and then slithered away
And Philly decided she must stop for the day.

She flew back home looking decidedly pale
And worried about that poor little snail.

She needn't have worried, the snail was all right
He was snuggly and cuddly and asleep for the night.

He hadn't had this much comfort before
And in ten seconds flat, he started to snore.

While Philomena slept she had a wonderful dream
Of chocolate and sweeties and cake and ice cream.

But most important came a thought from above,
It wasn't a house, she wants someone to love.

One day Philomena met a handsome young elf
She loved him at once, and not just for his wealth.

For he was a prince, brave Errol by name,
So Philly set out, his brave heart to claim.

Now Errol liked Philly the moment they met
But his dad always said, "Son, play hard to get."

When you choose a wife, she must be pretty and kind
So Errol would always keep that in mind.

But Philly was different, Errol swallowed his pride
And said, "Dearest Philly, will you be my bride?"

Philomena was happy, as pleased as could be
So she giggled prettily and sat on his knee.

Errol's mum wasn't happy and she told his dad
She'd chosen him another bride and was ever so mad.

Her face turned to purple, "It really won't do."
And with a look of fury, she waved her wand and flew.

The old king thought, "That's it for a week,
If she acts like the last time, she'll hardly speak."

The king didn't like her bride choice for Errol
But when the queen got mad they were all in grave peril.

The king told the couple, "The queen won't let you wed,
The marriage can't be," and he went home to bed.

Our sad Philomena went back home distraught,
She sat and she cried, she was really quite fraught.

What she didn't know was that if your heart is kind,
Nasty people can't harm you, so you really shouldn't mind.

Meanwhile, the nasty elfin queen was so cross she didn't see
The big, black dog in front of her, he thought she was a flea.

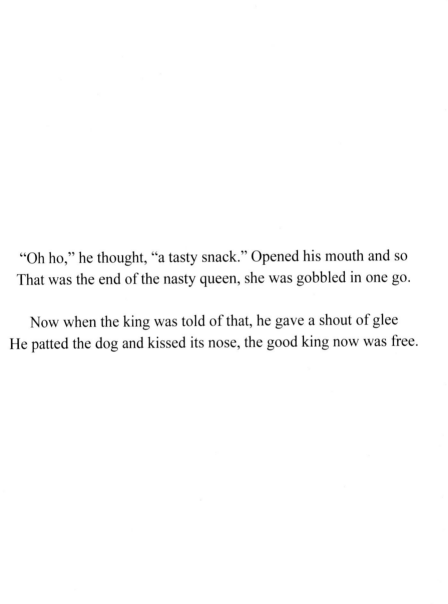

"Oh ho," he thought, "a tasty snack." Opened his mouth and so
That was the end of the nasty queen, she was gobbled in one go.

Now when the king was told of that, he gave a shout of glee
He patted the dog and kissed its nose, the good king now was free.

And so were Errol and Philly,
who got married with much laughter.

They lived in a castle,
had loads of fun and lived happily ever after.